CAMPUS
queen

I0619334

HALLIE
BENNETT

BOOKS BY THIS AUTHOR

For Type A personalities and the people who offer support and balance in their lives.

PROLOGUE

JOEL

"LAST PROJECT BEFORE graduation. Get excited!" I plop down beside Kenzie in the library, tossing my backpack onto the table. For four years, we've been paired together for everything from science experiments to history presentations because of our last names—Beecham and Beechman—and this is our final assignment. The professors must find it amusing to stick Type-A Kenzie with me, a total slacker and class clown, because it's the only explanation for why we've been stuck together for so long, despite the obvious mismatch.

"Are you actually going to contribute this time?" Kenzie's snarky reply rolls right off me, and I shrug nonchalantly.

"I'm here, aren't I?"

She rolls her eyes with a huff and makes a show of shoving my backpack off the table while snagging the textbook underneath it. The lightweight mesh material thumps to the carpet with barely a sound—its nearly empty contents a testament to my lack of preparedness.

"Your presence isn't as useful as you think it is, unless you actually apply yourself to the work." A worksheet slides across the wooden tabletop. "Here, this should be easy enough for you."

Other people might find Kenzie's snide attitude insulting, but it doesn't bother me. I hate studying and schoolwork. Kenzie loves that shit. So, if she's upset that I don't pull my weight when we're partnered together, I figure it's her right. After all, she's still getting me a good grade.

"Yes, your majesty." I wink and tug the question-filled sheet closer. It's no secret that Kenzie rules a certain part of campus like a royal queen. *She even has a king by her side to do her bidding*, I muse, thinking about how her and Kyle direct campus events like a power couple straight out of the corporate world.

They need to fucking loosen up.

Especially Kenzie.

In all the time I've known her, she's never been anything but perfect and in control. Perfect grades. Perfect behavior. *Except when it comes to me.* Whenever we're near, she can't resist dropping her guard to voice her perpetual frustration with my academic failings, and it's the only time I see the fiery core she hides behind a sturdy wall of control.

Wonder how deep it goes...

The familiar scent of vanilla tickles my nose, and I peek over at Kenzie's bent head studiously scribbling across her worksheet with neat penmanship. Is she fucking that Kyle guy? Does she show him her passionate side?

No way.

Because despite lush curves that promise comfort, her entire body is rigid and stiff with tension. I can't imagine she lets loose with him, or else Kenzie should be way more relaxed than she is.

"Do you need help with something?"

Fuck.

She caught me staring at her... again.

"Nah, I'm good. Just thinking." Kenzie snorts at the obvious lie but continues with her work, while I drag my focus away to one of the library windows looking over a pond at the edge of campus. My fascination for Kenzie has grown this year, and I don't know why. She hasn't changed—still a curvy little bundle of uptight rules. Yet, every now and then, I can't help watching her, intent on figuring her out.

A stupid endeavor.

After graduation, we'll go our separate ways and probably never see each other again.

What's it matter if I can't figure out one woman?

CHAPTER ONE

KENZIE
TEN YEARS LATER

"KENZIE, YOU'RE MEETING with tour leaders tomorrow morning, right?" Ms. Anderson hands over a manila folder as I set aside the misshapen centerpiece I'm fixing for tonight's cocktail party—the kick-off event for my class reunion during Homecoming Weekend. Ten years removed from attending Trinity College, and I still fall into my old role of leadership without a hitch: perfecting small details, organizing volunteers.

Guess being class president three years in a row sticks with you.

"Yep." I flip through the folder, seeing a list of group leaders along with a campus map highlighting suggested information to share. "All the volunteers are confirmed, so tours should run smoothly."

"Excellent! Thanks for offering to organize those. You're the best addition we've had to the alumni committee in a long time." Ms. A smiles and pats my shoulder before bustling away, leaving me with a glow of pride at her compliment, until Ashley Sims saunters up with her boyfriend, waving a full glass of champagne in the air with a knowing look.

"Here, here! All hail Queen Kenzie, the most organized, the most knowledgeable—the most likely to take over when you inevitably fuck up." Always eager for attention, Ashley's loud voice carries throughout the room, and the folder in my hand crinkles under the force of my grip as people stare at us.

Clearly, someone's enjoying the cocktails...

Laughing awkwardly at Ashley's embarrassing proclamation, I turn to finish adjusting the flowers for the table's centerpiece, trying to focus on Ms. A's words instead of Ashley's. Because it feels good knowing how much the alumni committee appreciates me. Like my tendency towards controlling things to ensure they're done right isn't a bad quality but an asset.

Not that it hasn't served me well for the past decade. I've built a thriving business that's all about organization and management. But sometimes, I wonder if I'm too overbearing or distrustful of others. Too afraid of others failing and letting me down. Even Ashley, a woman I haven't seen in years, remembers how disciplined I am.

Not like you don't have a reason to be.

From flaky family members to irresponsible co-workers, I've had my fair share of disappointment in life. So, what's wrong with trying to avoid more of the same?

It can be a lonely and daunting road attempting to achieve perfect outcomes.

Though it wasn't always.

When I was a student, I thought I'd met my match here at Trinity—someone to trust, someone I could rely on for help if necessary. Someone who never dropped the ball. Or made me regret trusting them.

In college, anyway. After graduation was a different story.

"Oh my gosh, they're so cute!" As if summoned by my thoughts, the man in question enters the room and is immediately called over by Ashley. His gaze meets mine briefly before joining us, and he introduces his husband Isaac, a slender man whose black hair blends in with his equally dark attire.

Kyle.

Former class vice president.

Ex-boyfriend.

Now, a married man.

Once upon a time, Kyle was the yin to my yang as we co-led study groups and planned events—the center of student activities and scholarly pursuits. Even the student body voted us "Most Likely to Become a Power Couple" in our senior yearbook. And as stupid as it sounds, I believed it.

How could I not?

We spent so much time together. We were compatible in so many ways.

Despite my practical nature, I daydreamed about a future with a man who understood me—accepted my Type A personality—and couldn't wait for us to start a life together after college.

Everything was great that first summer when we officially became an item.

Until Kyle sat me down one night and explained how things weren't working between us.

How he didn't want to be with a carbon copy of himself.

"Nice to meet you all, finally," Isaac says, a tentative smile shaping his thin lips. "Kyle's been regaling me with stories about everyone."

"All good, I hope!" Ashley titters, and it's obvious she's already verging on tipsy with her enthusiasm. For his part, her boyfriend seems to be taking it in stride.

Glancing between Kyle and Isaac, I contemplate our past. If I had to do it all over again, I wouldn't waste so much time dreaming and building up a relationship. I would've kept things professional. Friendly. Like I do now with anyone I work with.

You mean with anyone you meet.

But I ignore the inner taunt—aware of my fear of heartbreak, of making a mistake again—yet unwilling to risk changing anytime soon.

You have a great life. You don't need a man, too.

"Of course." Isaac faces me with an open expression and adds, "Especially about Kenzie. To hear him tell it, you two ruled campus as honorary king and queen."

"President and vice president. We're a democratic state." The words sound bitchier than I intend, so I force a smile and raise my champagne flute in a gesture of goodwill. "But he's right. Our class wouldn't have survived without us organizing events or running around in the background, so everything went off without a hitch."

Kyle cuts in. "Kenzie more than me. She was the real treasure. I just helped."

"Don't sell yourself short," I say, surprised by his comment. We shared the same responsibilities, and I always knew I could rely on Kyle to get things done. He was one of the few people I trusted to do what he said he'd do.

Honestly, it's what attracted me the most—the fact that he was trustworthy and reliable.

"Aww, that's sweet. I'm glad there's no hard feelings between you two." Ashley's eyes glaze over as she studies Kyle and me. "Most Likely to Become a Power Couple. And now you're married to Isaac while Kenzie's still single…" A suspicious gleam of tears appears, and it's time for me to bow out—I can't deal with Ashley's theatrics tonight.

"But we're all happy, and that's what counts. Besides, most of us didn't fulfill our prophetic legacies." Draining the last drop of alcohol from my glass, I back away from the table with a gesture of farewell. "I think I just saw Emily come in, and it's been forever since we've caught up. I'll talk to you guys later."

And I make my getaway—bypassing tossed out greetings and smiles—to sidle out the exit, needing fresh air.

That's the worst of it. Now you can enjoy the rest of your weekend without worrying about awkward introductions.

Kyle and I will still see each other. After all, he's one of the guides tomorrow, but at least we got that first meeting out of the way. And it wasn't terrible. Kyle was nice. Isaac was friendly. All in all, we're grown-ups who haven't been in each other's lives for a decade. We're being mature by moving on with our lives.

Even if *my* moving on hasn't involved love and marriage.

You don't need a man, I reiterate as my favorite spot on campus comes into view—the whitewashed gazebo set in a small pond.

A perfect refuge from the cocktail party.

CHAPTER TWO

JOEL

WHAT THE HELL ARE YOU doing?

When I decided to make this year's Homecoming Weekend and class reunion the location of my apology tour, I didn't expect it to entail following one curvy woman in the dark to the secluded campus pond. But with Kenzie's departure from the cocktail party and my determination to make things right with as many people tonight as possible, this seemed like the only option, despite the autumn chill clinging to my cheeks.

Sighing, I ask the question I've berated myself with since the moment I decided to attend this class reunion: *Why did I have to be such an ass in school?*

Because you were young and stupid and only cared about having fun.

Late-night parties. Skipping classes. Or goofing off when I did attend.

College was awesome.

Until the medical school I managed to get into with piss poor grades gave me a wakeup call. No one likes a slacker or a class clown who wastes time. They especially don't like it in future doctors. It took all my willpower to buckle down and actually contribute to discussions, do the hard work of learning.

But it's paid off now that I'm a pediatrician in my family's practice. However, it also means I realize how badly some people suffered here because of me. Which is why I'm following Kenzie.

I was the dick who barely lifted a finger to help her on class projects, while her work ethic and intelligence benefited me as she earned us good grades. At the time, I knew it wasn't right but enjoyed her snappy reactions to my bad behavior, along with the line of straight As I got. As an adult, though, I see how I should've done better, which makes an apology absolutely necessary.

Kenzie sits on the top step leading into the wooden gazebo, and I carefully step into the moonlight, letting her see me as I cross the wooden bridge leading to her perch.

"Hey." I offer a short wave of greeting before stopping and jumping into my spiel. "I'm not sure you remember me, but I'm Joel Beecham and we used to be partnered in class a lot."

"I remember." She leans back on her hands, head tilting to the side—clearly trying to figure out what I want. "Hard to forget the guy who frustrated you at every turn by doubling your workload during team projects."

Fuck, she still seems pissed.

"Right..." My stomach twists with shame, and I run a hand through my hair, grimacing at the uncomfortable situation my past self's put me in. "That's why I followed you out here. I want to apologize. I'm sorry for being a lazy asshole and putting so much on you. It wasn't fair, and you were kinder than you needed to be because you never did shoddy work. My best grades were because of you. So, I owe you a thank you along with an apology."

There. Mission complete.

Kenzie remains quiet as silver moonlight crisscrosses over her body, and it hits me how beautiful she is. Sapphire velvet outlines her curves, the deep vee of her neckline revealing bountiful breasts that somehow dodged my notice before. Has she always been this sexy?

I remember observing her in secret. Remember the fascination she held for me. Even recall thinking she looked soft. But I always rationalized it as natural curiosity, nothing more.

Obviously, you were wrong in more ways than you knew back then.

"Thanks for apologizing albeit ten years too late, but I appreciate the gesture."

"You're welcome." Duty done, I should leave, but then Kenzie shivers and I have an excuse to stay—to explore an attraction that's laid dormant for a decade. Shaking off my coat, I hurry forward and hand it to her. "Here, looks like you need this more than me at the moment. You're not exactly dressed for cooler weather."

She thankfully takes my offering and wraps it around her shoulders, huddling in the warm wool. "That's what happens when I make spur of the moment decisions. Which is why I avoid them usually." The mumbled addition at the end amuses me because from what I remember about Kenzie, she was the definition of responsible and prepared. Always had her schoolwork completed to perfection. Ran every campus event with precision.

"So, what happened? Why the sudden bolt outside?"

It's a toss-up whether she'll answer since we're not really friends, but she surprises me. "Needed a break from some people. Like my ex-boyfriend and his husband."

A vague memory of her and a nerdy looking guy comes to mind. Attached at the hip, every student-led activity featured the two of them together, working side by side. I always wondered if they dated, too.

"I get it. Break-ups are tough, and to learn your boyfriend's gay can't be easy."

Kenzie shakes her head in denial. "I knew Kyle was bisexual. That's not why we broke up or what bothers me. We dated for a few months after college because we got along so well. Truthfully, I was more convinced of our compatibility than he. Everything fell apart, though, when he decided we were too much alike. He wanted more of a counterbalance in his partner, which I understand. It's just not how I saw life going relationship-wise, and it sucks facing that reality surrounded by people who know our past."

"I see... So, he's here with his counterbalance and you're..." Single? Divorced? I'm itching to know if she's got a man in her life.

"Alone."

A wealth of discouragement lives in that one word.

Moving to sit beside her, I bump her shoulder with mine. "Cheer up, buttercup. You're not the only one." I've been single for a while, too, and the sheer number of couples dominating the cocktail party hit me in the gut from my first step inside the room. She must've felt the same thing ten times deeper with the presence of her ex and his spouse.

And a crazy idea pops into my head. "But maybe that can change for this weekend."

"What do you mean?" Skepticism furrows her brow as distrust radiates between us.

"We're both single. You need a distraction from Kyle, and I need to make up for years of mistreating you. Why don't we kill two birds with one stone and spend the weekend together?"

"Are you out of your mind? We're strangers, and the little I remember about you isn't positive." Kenzie jerks to the side and stares me down with blue eyes filled with incredulity. "An apology is one thing, but I'm not even sure I like you."

My hands lift in supplication. "Fair enough. But if you give me a chance, I'll guarantee a fun weekend where you don't have to face Kyle and his husband or any other uncomfortable situation alone. It can be platonic companionship or a guilt-free fling to provide a pleasurable distraction. It's up to you." Nowhere in my apology tour did I plan for an affair with a former classmate—let alone Kenzie Beechman—but with our past partially sorted out and this sudden burst of desire for her generous curves hardening my cock, I'm not about to miss an opportunity for some casual fun.

I might have become less of an ass with age, but I still enjoy a good time. Especially when it includes a gorgeous woman.

"So, what do you say?"

CHAPTER THREE

KENZIE

THIS MAN IS RIDICULOUS.

Bold.

Wild.

Am I seriously contemplating his suggestion?

For four years, Joel was the bane of my existence during group projects. He rarely showed up to class, never contributed to the workload. And there wasn't a thing I could do about it. The one time I mentioned changing partners, my professor denied me and tried to spin my dilemma into a learning situation on how to work with others.

"How can I be sure you'll hold up your end of the bargain? Previous experience says otherwise." Maybe seeing happy couples has affected me more than I thought because I never would have unloaded so much personal information on him otherwise. Plus, the idea of letting go for a few days and stockpiling pleasure-filled memories for future responsible me doesn't sound half bad. I may not need a man in my life—I'm great at taking care of myself—but that doesn't mean I'm too stubborn to turn down an opportunity for sex without the potential of heartbreak.

Abstinence has been my life for years as I've carefully avoided romantic entanglements, not quite cavalier enough to sleep with a partner without an emotional bond. But perhaps Joel's the perfect compromise. Nothing serious will form between us, so I'll be safe. And I know him well enough to have a connection, even if it's as tenuous as a spider's web.

"Care for a preview? Platonic or friends with benefits, just say the word, and I'll prove myself."

"Friends with benefits." The decision blurts out without a second thought and with shockingly little judgment. What happens on campus stays on campus, right?

"Excellent choice." He grins, a charming flash of white teeth and boyish enthusiasm. "How about a kiss for starters?"

Inhaling a lungful of crisp fall air, I let the shock of cold settle my nerves and nod.

Time to be reckless.

Responsibilities be damned... at least for now.

"Best make it good," I warn, "Or else our deal will end with it."

"Challenge accepted."

His hands encircle my waist as he hoists me onto his lap, my legs spreading over his thighs and exposing my lace panties to the zipper of his pants. "Whoa." My nails dig into his shoulders for security, and I struggle to orient myself after the abrupt movement. "Warn a girl next time." Though color me shocked that Joel has strength enough to drag me around like a plaything.

It's surprisingly hot.

"Noted," he says before wrapping a hand in the neat bun of hair at the nape of my neck and urging me forward without preamble.

The kiss is hard. Dominant. Not what I would've expected from Joel, and definitely unlike any first kiss I've ever had.

Not that I've had many, but they're usually tentative and controlled—not forceful and rough.

A heavy sigh stalls in my chest. Looks like I'll need to show him what to do here, too. Untangling myself from him, I loosen my grip on his shoulders and smooth languid circles over his chest, trying to convey the message to slow down. To rein it in instead of blasting off like a rocket.

"What are you doing?" he asks, amusement trickling into his voice.

"Showing you how to kiss the correct way."

The trickle becomes a river as Joel releases a hearty laugh, and I frown. Geez, he can't even take seduction seriously.

"Obviously, this is a mistake," I mutter. Scolding myself for believing this guy could help me in any sort of way this weekend, I quickly try to stand. This is my sign to suck it up and go back to the cocktail party, which has probably become the dinner by now, and forget about this strange interlude.

"Hang on." Joel's arms tighten around my waist, halting my progress. "You can't quit on me, yet. Especially since you haven't given me a fair shot."

"I let you kiss me." I point out with a roll of my eyes. And he failed the test.

"For two seconds before you tried taking control." His rebuttal hangs in the air, but there's no use denying the truth. I had to take over. "I know you're used to controlling everything and making sure it's perfect, but in this? With us? I'm in charge. You can have your way any other time."

"Well, if I don't like what you're doing, I'm not going to just accept it."

"How do you know what you'll like if you shut it down too soon?" His eyes soften slightly at my mutinous glare. I may have agreed to try this arrangement, but I'm not a pushover. "Look, I'm not opposed to trying what you want. You're used to things a certain way, and I understand. We like to stick with what we know, but I'd like to try my way first. Compromise, okay?"

His comment about sticking to the familiar rubs me the wrong way. Makes me feel like an old woman who refuses to learn or adapt. Makes me feel like I'm no fun at all, and I hate that perception.

"Fine." I can be flexible. I can adapt. My eyes close in preparation for another attack of his lips, but instead he nips me on the chin with his teeth. My eyes snap back open. "Hey! I said, fine. You don't have to punish me for voicing my opinion."

"I'm not." Joel shrugs, a mischievous gleam playing about his features. "I just wanted a bite." Then his mouth drops to nibble along my neck, sucking hard at random intervals until he reaches my cleavage—ensuring I don't return to the dinner tonight because my skin will be marked by him.

By love bites.

Hickeys.

Marks no one's ever given me before.

"Sorry if I caught you off guard earlier, but I thought it best to show you exactly what you'll be getting into this weekend." Another lick and rough suctioning on the side of my breast, the blazing trail leading to my nipple. "My days can be stressful, and

I'm guessing yours can be, too. Sex is my escape. Where I prefer to work out every strain and worry with vigorous fucking. That means I take what I want—no holds barred—and give it back tenfold. Slow and tender isn't out of the question, but it's not my default."

Well, that explains a lot.

With a swift drag of his hand, Joel shifts my dress and bra to the side, exposing my breast to the night chill before the heat of his mouth draws it between his teeth, and my body jumps at the contact. A breathy gasp fogs the air as he works the sensitive flesh with his tongue, the large hands at my hips pushing me down on his erection in a grinding motion.

This is more than I expected.

More than a simple kiss to seal our deal.

It's a blatant showcase of ownership to prove who's in charge, and the knowledge is headier than I ever could've dreamed. Like Joel's tapped into my deepest fantasy of having someone else be the boss for once. For someone else to guarantee things turn out alright.

Sex in the past has been perfunctory. Lackluster. It fell on my shoulders to pleasure my partner and myself.

But Joel's having none of it.

And I'm not quite sure how to handle the feeling of freedom.

CHAPTER FOUR

JOEL

KENZIE TASTES DELICIOUS, and it's a good thing I didn't know this about her in college or else she would've had a hard time doing our school projects with my hands and mouth caressing every inch of her body whenever possible.

Another reason I should've paid better attention in school.

"I'm gonna eat you up, buttercup." I whisper against the crook of her neck before easing her clothing back in place. "But you're gonna have to wait a little while longer." Better to leave her wanting tonight. Let her think about our deal and wonder what it'll be like between us because I sure as hell will be. With her tendency to lead, she's like a wild horse waiting for a strong enough hand to tame her—to not let her run roughshod.

It's kind of like my patients. The kids can be overexcited and stubborn, but once I've earned their trust, they settle down and allow me to do my job.

While Kenzie's far from being a child, she has the same tenacity of spirit that requires an understanding but firm guiding hand. My affinity for dominance in the bedroom baffled previous girlfriends—such a contrast from my easygoing personality, apparently—but my gut's telling me it's exactly what Kenzie needs.

"What... What are you doing?" Disoriented with arousal, she blinks up at me in confusion as I gently return her to the step beside me and stand.

"I've got a couple more people to apologize to tonight if I'm going to focus on you for the rest of the weekend." *A pleasurable reward for good behavior*, I muse, motivated to make my amends as quickly as possible. *Starting with my former roommate, Liam.*

"So, you're just leaving?"

"For now. But don't worry, we're not done yet." I can't resist cupping her cheek and swiping a thumb over her kiss-swollen lips. "I'll find you tomorrow, buttercup."

I guarantee it.

AS SUSPECTED, IT ISN'T difficult finding Kenzie the next day. One question of a tee-shirt clad volunteer leads to the administration building where I find her finishing a meeting with campus tour leaders, sending them off with their instructions like a good little general directing her troops.

I vaguely recognize some of the volunteers, including the guy I'm ninety-five percent sure is Kenzie's ex. His hair's neatly parted to the side while black glasses lend an intellectual air to his demeanor. He stops to say something to Kenzie before leaving, and it's easy to see them as a couple with their twin studious expressions.

A spark of jealousy flares up unexpectedly, and my jaw tightens in agitation. Not so much because I think their relationship will magically reignite—the man's married, after all—but seeing Kenzie's type and knowing I'm definitely not it.

Yeah, I pulled myself together enough to become a doctor, but outside of the medical sphere, I'm still a big kid at heart. I like to joke around and have fun, even if it means putting myself on display for a laugh—something I doubt Kyle's ever done in his life. He and Kenzie are buttoned-up, mature adults.

Though, I'm banking on Kenzie releasing her wild side this weekend, with my help, of course.

"Good morning! I brought breakfast." Holding a box of donuts aloft, I offer her a choice of the four drinks I ordered, since I wasn't sure which kind she'd like.

"Oh, wow... Thank you." She reads the haphazard labels on each drink before choosing a hot caramel macchiato. "You didn't have to get me anything, but it's definitely a godsend. I wasn't able to eat anything this morning before meeting with everyone."

"I figured you might be too busy to grab something. You were always on the go during college, and not much has changed, I see." We settle on a bench in the hallway, each snagging a donut—Kenzie, a jelly-filled one, while I scoop out the lone donut with chocolate icing. I take the remaining three drinks from her, pick the plain black coffee for myself, and place the rest beside me on the floor.

"Hmm... I guess you're right." She licks a smear of purple jelly off her lips with an adorable little hum of delight, and I scald my tongue with the large gulp of coffee I take to distract myself from the pretty sight. Shit, she can't be making eating donuts sexy. We're in the administration building, for crying out loud.

A rickety old building full of dusty textbooks and our former superiors. Nothing about this place screams romantic or seductive or *fuck me in the hallway*, yet here I am, nursing a growing erection because Kenzie innocently licked her lips.

"How'd you know where I was?"

I'm thankful for the opportunity to focus on anything but her mouth and my cock, so I launch in the short tale before asking what her plans are for the rest of the day. Because I know she's got to be involved with something else.

My girl thrives on running things.

My girl?

"I'm driving one of the school vans, so my afternoon's booked. But you're welcome to join, if you weren't already planning to go, that is. Plus, Kyle's the other driver, which means we can put your plan in action—sticking together amid all these happy couples."

The obstacle course. The bonding experience off campus. Right.

My brain tries to concentrate while thoughts of *my girl, mine* ignite like a damned fireworks show on the Fourth of July. I can't fall for her. Kenzie doesn't belong to me. We have three fucking days together before heading home, and then what?

We try the long-distance thing?

If you have to.

Fuck, fuck, fuck.

My mind, my body, and my heart are all spitting out different wants and needs. It's a fucking shitstorm rolling around in my gut, and she has no idea as she stares at me expectantly, waiting for an answer.

This afternoon. Our agreement.

Take it one step at a time, and you'll figure this out.

Tossing back another volcanic swig of coffee, praying the burning pain brings some clarity, I choke out three words. "Sounds like fun."

CHAPTER FIVE

KENZIE

HOURS LATER, I REGRET my decision to scale the eighty-foot-tall obstacle course with only a harness and tiny clip keeping me from plummeting to my death on River Sports' Sky Trail. Balance beams, zig zags of ropes, and other Fear Factor-like challenges lie between me and the free fall jump at the top, and I'm cursing Trinity for thinking this makes for a good bonding experience.

I would've been just fine safely on the ground, chatting with former classmates—no need for scaling a freaking steel monolith.

"Come on, you can do it. You're close to the end now." Joel holds the swaying bridge as steady as he can from his position on the opposite side as I gingerly hop across planks laid at odd intervals. It's our last obstacle before reaching the top, and I have to give him credit because he's being incredibly patient and helpful. The Joel I knew before wouldn't have thought twice about shaking the unsteady bridge to scare me and to get a laugh out of others.

Thank goodness, he's matured.

More than I realized.

I steal a quick peek at his toned arms braced along the ropes, his muscular legs providing a firm foundation of support, and can't help the flutter of butterflies swooping around in my belly. He's grown into a man—a fully-developed male in his prime. My body knows it, recognized it last night at the gazebo, but now my mind's catching up.

"Good job, buttercup." Joel reaches for my hand and pulls me onto the steady platform at the end of the bridge. Somehow, I made it across without much thought, too caught up in fantasizing about hard muscles and how they felt beneath me.

Geez, get a grip, girl.

"Thanks... Are you sure you don't want to jump down with me?" We've made it to the end of the course, and there are only two ways down: by jumping off a ledge or gliding down a ginormous slide. Since I've never experienced the feeling of weightlessness before—no matter how brief it'll be—I opted for the free fall.

Joel watches one of our classmates, Monica, step off the extended scaffolding to land safely a few seconds later on the target mat below and scrunches his nose in refusal. "Nah, I'm good. The slide's more my speed."

"Like a kid at the playground," I tease but urge him towards the slide as I get in line for the jump. The sign at the start of the course listed height and weight requirements which I double-checked to make sure I was well within range of. Having experienced an embarrassing moment at a theme park five years ago when I couldn't fit in the regular rollercoaster cart and had to be moved to the plus-sized one, I never want to go through something like that again. Hell, I still scold myself for not checking the requirements for that particular ride years later. I don't need another humiliating experience haunting me, too.

The line moves forward as Josh Parker prepares to jump and asks a million questions while getting hooked into the bungee cord. I see Joel already standing below, staring up with a hand over his head to block the sunlight. Waving, I force a brave smile as the gap between me and him registers.

The jump didn't look so bad earlier but now that I'm next to be secured into the harness, fear creeps in with a sick tightening in my gut. What am I doing? I could get hurt. *Die!* This thing could break under my weight and then what? I'll plunge to my death in front of a group of old classmates and a bunch of strangers.

You can't back out now. You said you'd do this, so you will.

A garbled yell rises from Josh as he takes a running leap into the air—a direct contrast to the safety operator's advice of stepping off the platform in a controlled-fashion—but despite the warning, the wild jump doesn't cause any issues. Josh lands on his feet and raises two fists in victory while another course employee unhooks him from the tether.

My turn.

"Ready?" A minute later, the safety instructor tugs on my harness ensuring its security, and I nod because I can't chicken out now. Josh just made a spectacle of himself flying off the edge like some kind of superhero, the least I can do is take one baby step off. Ten seconds of bravery.

You've got this.

Inhaling a deep breath, I count to three then exhale, walking out into thin air. Gravity quickly drags me back to earth for an exhilarating moment—my stomach flying up to my chest in a strange ticklish sensation—until an audible snap sounds from above, and my semi-controlled descent goes wildly off course. A yelp of terror erupts from my swinging body as I desperately hold onto the bungee cord, narrowly missing slamming into a steel beam.

Gray concrete flies into view, and I brace for a hard landing when someone crashes into my flailing body, sending us rolling to the ground in a tangled heap. A firm chest cushions my head, rampant beating matching the erratic pace of my own heart while I struggle to catch my breath.

"Kenzie, are you alright?" It's Joel. He's the one who saved me, and I've never been so glad to see the man in my life.

Before I can reply, strangers pull me off of him—people in medic gear tossing out a barrage of questions as they poke and prod—but I'm incapable of uttering more than one-word answers as shock sets in.

For all my caution, I still could've been seriously injured.

Despite doing everything right.

Checking the obstacle's height and weight requirements. Listening to the safety trainer's directions.

And none of it mattered.

Everyone else was safe before me, and once they check the line again, I'm sure those after me will be, too. Yet, I'm the one sitting on hard concrete, overwhelmed by strangers touching me and trying not to have a panic attack.

Tears blur my vision. Not so much from physical pain, but from the futility of it all. I was careful and smart, and it didn't mean a damn thing.

Don't be stupid. Pull yourself together; you can't cry right now.

Glancing upward, I rapidly blink away the threat of waterworks, willing them to wait until I'm in my hotel room, free to break down in privacy. Even seeing Kyle yesterday and being reminded of my failure didn't make me cry. Guess a near-death experience was all I needed to push me over the emotional edge.

"Looks like you sustained some minor bruising from the yank of the harness, but otherwise, I think you'll be okay. Just take it easy for the rest of the day, okay?" The kind medic pats my arm before packing her things into a red bag, and I hear Joel reassure her from his position next to me.

"I'll watch over her. I'm a doctor, so she's in good hands."

A doctor? My brain struggles to compute the slacker image of Joel with that of a doctor, especially through the fog of shock and self-recrimination clouding my mind.

"Yep, I'm a pediatrician." I must have voiced my doubt aloud as he answers, taking hold of my hand and massaging the reddened palm—evidence of my death grip on the bungee cord earlier. Swallowing thickly at the sight, I count my breaths, praying the simple act calms my nerves.

"It wasn't easy," he continues. "You know I wasn't motivated in undergrad, but eventually I found my focus. My family owns a practice in our hometown, and I always knew I wanted to join them someday. Post-grad was a wake-up call. If I wanted to work with my family and help kids, I needed to grow up and focus on what mattered. I kept that front of mind throughout school and my residency."

Interesting.

A responsible and hardworking Joel. Who would've thought?

"If you're ready to walk, we can get out of here." He stands and offers a hand to me. "Go somewhere more private. But only when you're ready. Don't push if you're not."

"Private sounds nice." A small group of people stand to the side watching us as if waiting for me to keel over suddenly from a delayed reaction to the fall. Escaping prying eyes is just what I need. Ignoring his hand, I lurch up from my sitting position, wobbling on rubbery legs and slamming a palm against the steel pillar I'd been leaning against for support.

Guess you should've accepted his help.

"Whoa, easy." Joel's arm circles my back, and he bends as if to swoop me up into a lift.

"Stop! What are you doing?" We form an awkward pretzel with my body stretching to avoid his approaching embrace. "I can walk. I just need a second."

"Don't force anything. That was a traumatic fall despite your minor injuries. Let me get you back to the van where you can rest." He tries again, and I wiggle in his arms like a worm on a fishing hook. I am not letting him carry me. It would be too humiliating.

"No, I'm fine. See?" I stiffen my muscles and step forward, heading towards the parking lot. "I appreciate the chivalry and all, but I doubt we would've made it far anyway. I'm not exactly a lightweight."

"Neither am I." Joel huffs, and my attention fastens on his broad shoulders and the muscles contracting under his tee. But despite his obvious strength, I'm not about to let him try lifting me for any distance. I've been embarrassed enough today, thank you.

Hell, I double-checked the weight limit for the obstacle course before ever snapping into the harness, and I still ended up on my butt. Granted, apparently Josh's wild antics before my jump are to blame for messing with the rigging, but who knows? Maybe my larger size exacerbated the problem.

We slowly make it to the school van where I gratefully sink into the driver's seat, resting my head against the padded back and closing my eyes in relief. Joel settles into the passenger seat, and it's a minute before I collect myself enough to continue our previous conversation, eager to move on from my fall and learn how he turned his life around so drastically.

"Tell me more about life after Trinity because I'm having a hard time envisioning you surviving medical school." With a turn of the key, I roll the windows down to let the cool fall breeze drift inside while we wait for everyone else to join us when the course closes in an hour.

"You're not the only one." Joel chuckles, reclining his seat back and propping an elbow against the door jamb. He shoots a boyish grin across the console, and my stomach tightens in awareness. He really is adorable. Words I never thought I'd say about Joel Beecham. "I was really lucky to be accepted into Fallon College of Medicine. No doubt my dad helped with his connection to the dean. Honestly, I thought I'd coast through because of that, but Dr. King quickly set me straight my first semester. Told me to shape up or ship out basically."

Doubt creases my forehead; it's difficult imagining a stern lecture having that much of an effect on Joel. Surely our professors at Trinity tried the same thing with less than stellar results. "And just like that you became the perfect student?" My voice drips with disbelief—there's got to be more to this story.

CHAPTER SIX

JOEL

"NOT QUITE PERFECT." *Far from it.* "I attended a bunch of study group sessions, even had a tutor for a semester. At times, my brain felt like it was going to melt with all the information being shoved into it every day. But like I said, joining my family's practice and helping kids became my top priorities. I focused on those two goals throughout my years at Fallon, through residency at St. Mary's Hospital, and it's gotten me to where I am today."

The early-setting sun shines into the van and highlights tiny dust particles in the air as I contemplate the path of my life so far. Ruminating on the past isn't exactly my favorite pastime—like Walt Disney said, *keep moving forward*—but it's interesting sharing with Kenzie.

I want to impress her with my improvements.

I want to prove I'm worthy of her time.

She stares out the windshield, her hands tinkering around with the steering wheel, and the dark red striping the palms bothers me. It matches the glimpse of red peeping from the collar of her tee where the bungee cord abraded her skin.

Watching her fall from below—with no way of stopping it—had frozen me in place with crushing fear, until the sight of her almost hitting a steel beam rocketed me into action. Kenzie landing in my arms safely, with only minor scratches and bruises, will forever be branded in my mind.

I'd never felt such an intense wave of relief in my entire life.

Oblivious to my observation, she asks another question—ever the curious woman who needs all the facts. The notion warms me from the inside out knowing she's curious about me. "Why pediatrics? I understand wanting to work with your family, but the choice of specialty isn't what I'd expect. Though, I never would've pegged you for a doctor at all, so any specialty would seem strange."

"That's an easy one. Kids are the best. I love hanging out with them because they tell you like it is. They're truthful, not bogged down by adult concerns. They're full of joy and playfulness, and I relate to their sense of fun." I shrug, remembering a discussion I had with my dad about a future in pediatrics. He'd had his reservations, as well. "My dad's a general practitioner. My mom's an OB-GYN, and my brother followed in Dad's footsteps. But working with adults never appealed to me. Too many bad interactions when I visited the practice growing up. It's just a different outlook on life."

Kenzie nods, her gaze fixated on the windshield, following the group of people heading towards us. "That makes sense. You're kind of a big kid yourself... or you were."

"I'm going to take that as a compliment."

We share a smile as the side door opens and our peers pile into the van, sweating and laughing. Naturally, the conversation shifts to hearing about everyone's experience on the obstacle course while Kenzie drives us back to campus. Anytime someone mentions her accident, she calmly directs the attention away from herself until its forgotten, clearly uncomfortable rehashing the scary moment, and I can't blame her.

If I never visit another adventure track like River Sports' Sky Trail, it'll be too soon.

White stadium lights from the soccer field brighten the evening as we park at the college forty-five minutes later, everyone separating into groups for the night—some heading towards the field while others search out food for dinner. Kenzie pulls out a tiny notebook to write down the mileage and gas used as the dim glow of the dashboard light highlights her elegant handwriting.

"You don't have to wait for me to finish this," she says, pausing her writing to glance over at me.

"Are you forgetting about our deal? We stick together this weekend, and since we're both free until tomorrow night's dance..." I snag her hand and turn it over to place a kiss on the inside of her wrist, carefully avoiding the ink point of her pen. "You're mine for the next twenty-four hours."

"Am I?" The husky note in her voice is the call of a siren from the sea, and I use my hold on her wrist to tug until she's within reach, our mouths meeting in the dark for a stolen moment of bliss.

Releasing her after a short nip to her bottom lip, my chin bobs up and down. "Yes, you are. Which is why we're returning to my hotel room when you're done here."

"Your room, huh?" She readjusts in her seat, and I wonder if she's as affected as I am by our kiss and the promise of tonight—my blood's heating in anticipation, my cock rallying for a night of fun. "That's probably a good thing, since I'm splitting hotel fare with a friend."

"Wanted that college experience again with roommates?"

"Oh, you know it." She grins then closes the little notebook with the van information and shoves it into the middle console. "Alright, we're good to go. I'll follow you in my car?"

"Sounds good," I say and hurry to my car, eager to get her alone and in my bed.

Throughout the brief drive to my hotel—hell, since last night's wild attraction to Kenzie flared to life—I fantasize about having her beneath me, reveling in her submission to my control in the bedroom. Because I know it's nothing she's ever done before. Kenzie doesn't loosen the reins for just anyone, only for people she trusts, and even then, I doubt it's easy.

But I'm going to prove she can trust me to take care of her needs.

I won't leave her disappointed or frustrated.

Never again.

Besides, I'm betting she's hiding a competency kink along with a side of submissive under all that rigid control, and the thrill of being the man to reveal that side of her is fucking catnip. The men of her past—Kyle included—obviously didn't know how to satisfy her well. Or at all.

That ends tonight.

CHAPTER SEVEN

KENZIE

JOEL'S HOTEL ROOM LOOKS similar to mine. Heavy brocade curtains, neatly-made bed—your standard room for travelers, and I'm thankful that he's located across the parking lot from where I'm staying. In case things turn sour, I have a quick getaway handy.

Though his confidence boosts my hope that tonight won't be a total failure. If what happened between us at the cocktail party or even in the van earlier is anything to go by, we definitely have chemistry. But I've been wrong before.

Don't think about Kyle.

Today had been surprisingly easy working with Kyle during the campus tours and seeing him at the obstacle course since he was the other van driver. The awkwardness I feared would appear never materialized, and Joel's presence wasn't needed so much as a distraction. He was just fun to hang out with, no agenda necessary. In fact, the entire day flowed perfectly until the accident, though I suppose my survival of that particular event bodes well for tonight, too.

You can only go up from here, right?

A tossed jacket flies by me while I survey the room. Joel's shoes and socks are removed, his shirt next as he yanks it over his head by the collar. Chiseled muscles and tan skin are shown to advantage under the soft light emanating from a desk lamp, the lone bright spot in the room, and I swallow the sudden thickness in my throat, forcing my lungs to keep working—releasing the breath stuck in my chest.

Has he always been this hot?

Was I really so blinded by Kyle that I ignored Joel?

To be fair, you were probably blinded by rage at Joel's apathetic attitude.

"On the bed. Naked." The firm command interrupts my musings as hesitation freezes my limbs.

"But we haven't kissed or anything... Shouldn't there be more before..." I gesture towards the bed. We'll get there eventually—sooner rather than later—but damn. I need to warm up first.

"What did I say?" One of his dark brows rises in admonishment, and he steps closer until we're chest to chest. "In the bedroom, I'm in control. Now, are you gonna behave and listen?"

I bristle at his tone, though my thighs clench in response, my head and body sending mixed signals. No one orders me around. Not because I'm intimidating, but because they know I don't need to be told to do things. I anticipate needs and complete tasks on my own. *Even during sex.* Previous sexual encounters where I had to guide the man while still requiring my own hand to orgasm.

Maybe it's time for a change.

Unzipping my jacket, I throw it next to Joel's on the desk chair and wiggle out of my remaining clothes before lying flat on the bed, breasts and pussy exposed to his heated gaze—his eyes never wavering from my movements during the entire strip show. *What show? You didn't even try to make it sexy.* But he doesn't seem to care, riveted by each swathe of skin revealed.

"You're fucking gorgeous, buttercup."

Four words, and the flush of hot arousal blazes across my skin, singing every nerve.

The shadows cast by the lamp must be working wonders for my curves because gorgeous isn't how I'd normally describe my body. Not that I spend too much time fighting my weight—my body type's been the same my whole life, and I don't foresee that changing anytime soon—but stretch marks and cellulite aren't a girl's best friend. Guys don't rave about those features when listing what they like in a woman.

So, it feels good to hear Joel's admiration.

Allows me to believe that I am sexy and gorgeous—even if it's just for tonight, just for him.

Contemplating how weird it'd be to thank him for the compliment, my thoughts fly in a different direction when I see him steal a rag from the closet and fold it into thirds before approaching the bedside.

"What's that for?"

"You, if you agree. We're improvising, but it works since you're new to this." The mattress dips under his weight as he sits and raises the folded white rag into view. "I want to cover your eyes so you only focus on what's happening and not on what you *think* should happen. But it's up to you."

No surprise he wants to limit my ability to voice objections. I've tried to backseat drive things between us from the start. Sparing a considering look at the clean cloth, I agree, "Okay... but I don't think it's long enough to tie around my head."

"That's alright. Gives you the power to shake it off if you need to." He pauses before lowering the makeshift blindfold. "Which reminds me. While we're not getting into anything super dangerous or anything, I think you should have a safe word. For my piece of mind, and so you know you have a way out if it becomes too much."

Good grief, this is getting serious.

Ironically, my friends and I had joked about what our safe word would be in a drunken conversation years ago. We'd watched the Fifty Shades of Grey trilogy for fun and got inspired to come up with our own. Guess the time's come to use it. "Popsicle."

An amused expression supplants his look of lust for a moment before he nods. "Okay. Popsicle it is then." Joel places the rag over my eyes blocking out most of the light.

And I wait.

Intrigued by what he'll do next.

The brush of his hand ghosts over my left breast, avoiding my nipple to travel lower over a round hip then further to tickle behind my knee. I jerk at the sensation but stay quiet, willing the words of direction swirling in my head to disappear. *As if you even know how to direct him.* Which is true.

My normal suggestions seem—basic?—compared to Joel's way of lovemaking. Not that I'm opposed to prolonged foreplay, but in my limited experience, the guy usually gets bored and tries to skip to the main event before it really has time to develop into any kind of desperate need on my part.

"Stop thinking so hard." Another caress follows his command. This time a lone fingertip circles my right nipple before sliding down the center of my chest and tracing the under curve of my belly. "Focus on the sensations in your body. How the rasp of my fingertips feels over your skin. The cool breeze blowing across your fevered flesh." His hypnotic baritone calms the chaos in my mind, and I wish the drone of the AC in the background would quiet down—one) because now that he's mentioned it, the chill is undeniable, and two) because I want to hear Joel's voice without interference.

"I thought you said you didn't do gentle," I say as his breath coasts along the crease between my thigh and pussy, and I strain to determine whether that extra something is finally his lips or just my imagination.

"I said it's not my default. But for now, you could use some gentleness. That harness did a number on your body, buttercup." I imagine wrinkles marring his forehead in concern to match the tone of his voice. "Purple and red dots are sprinkled in haphazard lines along here. A smattering of bruises coming to the surface." A warm palm rests over my heart and the shock of heat draws a gasp of surprise. It's in direct contrast to the iciness of the AC.

Why does he have the temperature set so low in autumn?

Does it matter when he's touching you like this?

"Could be worse. At least the harness did its job of saving me from a worse fate."

"True... Open your mouth." The command confuses me, but I comply, wondering if this is a weird segue into a kiss—something we haven't done since we entered his room. Instead, his thumb presses into my tongue, leaving a faint taste of salt, before it swipes a line over a budded nipple.

The wetness immediately evaporates, and the resulting bite sends an immediate reaction to my dampening pussy, heightening my awareness of the frigid caresses of air. I know blocking one sense like my sight increases the sensitivity of others, but I'm not quite prepared for the overall effect when it comes to sex. Every delicate sensation builds upon the other. Sharpens my need into a fine point that centers on my core. All I crave is focused attention on my clit or the rough thrust of his cock filling that achy spot inside.

But Joel keeps lightly running his hands over random spots on my body—my neck, thigh, the delicate bones of my ankle—until I can't resist arching into his touch, silently urging him to do more.

When he doesn't take the hint, I grumble, "How much longer are you going to make me wait?"

Because I get it.

He knows what he's doing. He doesn't need my help. And the realization of his competency chips away at the lingering sense of caution in my mind, freeing me to completely submit to his wishes a little bit more.

"Patience, buttercup." The dark chuckle I hear shouldn't arouse me, but damn, he sounds like a sexy villain playing with his prey. Something the old Joel never could've pulled off—he was firmly sidekick material in college. "You'll get your reward soon enough."

Soon needs to be now, I inwardly grouse, teetering on a fine line of sexual frustration.

Suddenly, a large hand wraps around my wrist and draws it up, careful not to disturb the rag cloaking his actions. "How do you feel about being tied up?"

"I get a say?" The bratty retort is spoken before I have time to second guess it, and a swat of retribution lands on my hip.

"Don't sass me. Or else I might decide to show you how little brats get disciplined." His hot breath at my ear has me squirming. I'm not a brat. I'm not immature or badly-behaved.

Ask anyone and they'll say I'm the antithesis of these things.

Then why am I so turned on by the thought of him punishing me?

"Now, tell me. Yes or no to being restrained?"

"Yes."

A rumble of approval vibrates through his chest to mine causing me to bow forward to keep contact with his body, but he moves away, breaking the connection, and I stifle a groan of disappointment. Like a petulant child not getting her way, irritation wells inside.

I'm not a brat, but he's making me into one.

Because I don't want to wait. I don't want to practice patience.

Here's a man who is pushing all my buttons, toying with my body like it's his personal plaything, and I want satisfaction.

Now.

Kyle would've been done and asleep by this time while I snuck my hand under the covers to finish myself, but Joel's different. Logically, I know he's working to build me up into the best orgasm I've ever had. Emotionally, though? I need the release. I need proof he won't just give up because it's taking too long.

I need absolute, irrefutable proof that I made the right decision agreeing to this weekend fling, that it's safe for me to not control everything. That Joel's changed and can be trusted.

A lot riding on a couple of orgasms.

It may be irrational, but it's how I feel.

Silky material slides over my wrist before it circles my other hand, tying me to a spindle in the headboard, and I'm immediately brought back to the moment.

Do what Joel said. Focus on what he's doing instead of spiraling in your head.

"Do you know why I think you need to be tied up, buttercup?" His nickname for me should probably annoy me or remind me of a Power Puff girl, but I like that he sees me as something sweet and delicate—adore that he cares enough to even use an endearment. In the past, men stuck with my name, just different variations like McKenzie or Kenz. Which never upset me, but it seems impersonal compared to Joel's moniker. Like they couldn't be bothered to dig below the surface and show they thought of me as more than just straightlaced Kenzie.

A little thing that makes a big difference.

"Because you're worried I'll try to take over again?" I venture, testing the bonds around my hands and finding them pleasantly loose, so if I really tried, I could break free. Not that I'm planning on it. There's something very liberating about knowing I'm at Joel's mercy. I'm not expected to perform or lead because I physically can't—my ability to control has been removed.

"Exactly." He urges my legs into a bent position, his weight bearing down on me until his mouth roughly draws my nipple between his lips and teeth, and the switch to dominant possession versus gentle persuasion almost has me climaxing right then. Moving to my other breast, Joel pinches the taut bud. "You're going to lie here and take everything I give you, knowing that you're mine to do with as I see fit. Your only requirement is to submit. Moan your pleasure. Scream my name. But remember who's fucking your curvy little body—me. I know exactly how to make you come until you won't be able to attend tomorrow's dance because your pussy's sore, your legs too weak. Understand?"

"Yes, yes, yes..." My last word ends on a hiss as Joel's body shifts lower, his warm skin rubbing against mine in a sinuous dance of seduction. The slow and steady portion of our night must be over because he buries his face between my thighs, and I have little time to react to the sudden overload of sensations.

One hand splays over my chest, continuing to tweak and tease my nipples into throbbing points, as his other hand presses down on my left thigh to give him more space to eat me out. A burning pressure emanates from the spot, and I vow to stretch more regularly so he can open me as wide as possible to lick and suck and fuck me senseless.

You planning on extending this past the weekend?

I ignore the question, unwilling to delve into what it means about my feelings for Joel.

"Damn, you're fucking delicious." A growl of hunger hums along my clit as he nestles himself deeper, the bristles of his five o'clock shadow scratching at the tender skin of my pussy. "If I'd known your cunt was this sweet in college, we would've flunked out because I would've had your legs wrapped around my head every single fucking day. The entire dorm floor would've been jealous, hearing your moans of pleasure—the slick, wet sound of me eating this juicy cunt."

His tongue glides inside my desperately grasping walls before retreating and repeating the rhythmic thrusting. I gasp for some much-needed air, swallowing hard. "I wouldn't have let you derail my grades so badly."

He pauses, and an embarrassing whine keens in my throat.

Come back.

"You wouldn't have had a choice when I chained you to my bed. Don't think I wouldn't have had you bound and spread before me like a damned buffet—a thousand times more delectable than anything I'd ever eaten in my life."

I whimper at the thought. Good thing we'll never know how I would've held up against his persistence because a niggling suspicion says I just may have given in.

CHAPTER EIGHT

JOEL

KENZIE'S MINE.

Mine.

For a usually laidback kind of guy, the possessiveness I feel towards her surpasses anything I've ever known. Its swift appearance belies the intense certainty in my gut that we're meant to be together. How twenty-four hours could bring such a drastic change to my life is beyond me, but I'm not questioning it.

Love's been elusive over the years. Not that I haven't been open to falling for someone or dedicated to making relationships work, but no one's ever felt right.

Except Kenzie.

She feels more than right.

She feels perfect.

From her cautious yet curious nature to the intoxicating sweetness of her cunt. Every inch of her calls to me, smooth curves molding to my rough edges in a mish-mashed puzzle.

"Mmm... Guess things worked out as they should have then." Kenzie's breathy words go in and out as her thighs flex around me. "We both safely graduated."

"If you say so. Personally, I prefer licking your pussy to studying for exams." To punctuate the point, I flick her glistening clit with my tongue, spelling MINE over the tender bud. Perhaps it's childish. The act of a caveman. But I don't give a fuck.

I plan on branding Kenzie as mine with every kiss, lick, and bite. I wasn't kidding about making her miss tomorrow's dance out of sheer exhaustion. But there's also another secret reason: because she has too many love marks to successfully hide. Not that I'd mind people seeing them. Good to let other men know where they stand—which is absolutely nowhere within a foot of her. However, Kenzie's an upstanding alum of Trinity, and I doubt she's comfortable enough broadcasting our night together to the entire campus.

The wooden headboard knocks against the wall as she strains against her bounds, her breathing becoming harsher as her hips buck into my mouth, and I know she's close to reaching her peak. *Needs just a little extra push.* My thumb and finger trap a rosy nipple in a firm grip, tightening the pressure to match the rough suction of my lips on her clit, furiously agitating it with the tip of my tongue, until a high-pitched cry rises from above and Kenzie shudders beneath me.

"Joel..."

Growling at the moan of my name, I don't let up the harsh pace, instead pushing harder, urging her higher. In the back of my mind, I wonder if it's too much too fast when she's not used to such treatment. *Kenzie has her safe word.* If it hurts or she's done, she knows to say it.

But my girl's not a quitter.

Another climax rips through her body as a flood of wetness drenches my mouth and chin. *Oh, fuck.* I grind my erection into the bed, aching for relief. I'm tempted to let myself go and come with her, but a stronger part of me wants to release inside of Kenzie for our first time together. So, I content myself with the rubbing friction of my jeans on the bed until my cock can be saturated in her hot slick.

It'll be well worth the wait.

After the last wave of her orgasm fades, I ease off Kenzie, and she mewls at the minor respite. Her makeshift blindfold lies on the pillow next to her, sweaty strands of hair clinging to her face and the pillowcase, as I carefully untie her wrists and massage the pinkened flesh.

"How do you feel?" I ask, eager to check in and assure that she's okay, but before she can reply, a loud growl emanates from her stomach, protesting our lack of dinner. Laughing, my hand rubs the soft skin of her belly. "Well, that answers my question. Does pizza sound good to you?"

Kenzie hums in approval, dragging the comforter over her shoulder and cuddling into my side. *Drowsy as a kitten.* I've never seen her this relaxed, and pride raises my feathers like a damn peacock because I'm the man responsible. Gingerly reaching across her for my phone on the nightstand, I search for the nearest pizza spot and quickly order from their menu.

Task done, I toss the phone aside, readjust my raging hard-on, and settle in beside Kenzie, stroking any part of her I can through the blanket. Her muscles are probably sore from the extended tension—despite her release—and it's important for me to alleviate residual pain.

A fist bangs on the door thirty minutes later, and it's jarring compared to the quiet oasis we're floating in. Rolling from the bed, I open the door to find our food in the hotel hallway, resting on a tiny cardboard stand. Contactless delivery for the win even if the floral carpet *is* sketchy with hundreds of strangers' footprints.

Pizzas hot in my hands, I shoot a quizzical glance Kenzie's way. "The desk or the bed?"

Sitting in the middle of the mattress, looking thoroughly fucked with her wild hair and flushed skin, I'm almost tempted to forgo dinner in favor of continuing our lovemaking. Except her stomach growls again, and I remind myself to not be an asshole.

"The bed. Easy and casual. Though you're overdressed." Her eyes drop to my jean-clad legs while she holds the comforter to her breasts, creating a deep vee of cleavage between the plump globes.

Dropping the pizzas next to Kenzie, I step back to shuck the denim as she opens a box and pulls out a pepperoni slice. "Dinner and a show." She winks before biting into the cheesy goodness.

"Does that mean I should turn around? Keep up the mystery?" If she's feeling playful, then I'm ready to join in. Giving her an exaggerated wiggle of my hips, I face the covered windows and undo the pants button and zipper, enjoying the light banter.

The jeans clear my ass, and I hear Kenzie's muttered, "Damn."

Hang on, buttercup. You ain't seen nothing yet.

I kick the pants aside and turn towards Kenzie, giving her the full view—though, I'm still wearing my boxer briefs—but that doesn't stop her gasp of "Double damn."

"Glad you approve." *Because I want to be the last cock you ever see.*

She pulls the food closer to make room for me on the bed as I sit across from her, stealing one of the cheese slices. We eat companionably in peaceful silence, though a world of communication transpires within our shared gaze. Curiosity. Anticipation. Surprise. Hesitation.

Studying her open expression, I test the waters with a question. "So, you know about my life after Trinity, but what about you? How has the golden girl gone on to rock the world?"

Covering a spate of coughing, she grabs one of the bottled waters lying on the bed. "Rock may be an exaggeration. But I've done okay. I started my own organizing company about five years ago, and it's really taken off lately since home organizing is trending. Thank you, Marie Kondo and the Home Edit." I don't recognize the names but raise a bottle of water in solidarity with her.

"I always knew you'd be successful in whatever you chose to do."

"Because I'm too controlling to let myself fail?"

"No, because you work hard, you're extremely smart, and you're a great leader. Everyone on campus knew that about you."

"Oh, well thank you." An endearing blush tinges her cheeks as a pleased smile shines back at me.

"You're welcome..." Chewing thoughtfully on a bite of seasoned crust, I mull over my next question before tossing it out, wondering how she'll react. "But now I've got to ask. Why are you so determined to control the outcome of things? There are lessons to be learned in failing or going off course, too."

I should know. I'm the fucking poster boy for going off course.

Kenzie sighs and wipes the excess grease off her fingers with a napkin—a slow and methodical practice as she considers how to answer. "It's more about being let down in the past by people. You included. I feel stupid when I trust someone to do something then they don't follow through. I feel like I should've been wise enough to know better. If I control things, then at least if something goes wrong, I can rightfully blame myself. Which is somehow better than feeling stupid about trusting the wrong person." She shrugs. "I don't know. It's a convoluted rationale that I realize needs altering."

I'm dying to ask about the people who've let her down. I hate being one of them, but I understand why I'm on the list. But who else is? Kyle? Other boyfriends? Or is she talking in general from personal relationships to business?

"Everyone makes mistakes." *Groundbreaking advice, Joel.* "That doesn't make you stupid. It just means you're human. But I'm sorry you've been disappointed so often; you don't deserve that kind of treatment. Again, I apologize for my part in it, too."

"Oh, you've gone above and beyond with your apology. Most don't provide earth-shattering orgasms." Then, out of nowhere, her nose wrinkles in disgust. "So, I wanted that to be sexy, but then I started thinking about everyone who's let me down. Some of those people include family and that would just be gross." She shudders, her mouth pinching at the corners, and I can't help but laugh at her expression.

"Buttercup, you are too fucking adorable for your own good."

Kenzie makes a face and flops back onto her pillow with a whoosh. "I'm too fucking analytical. I overthought a simple statement and made it weird."

"Hey." Moving the pizza boxes to the floor, I crawl up her prone form until we're face to face. "You didn't make it weird. That's just where your mind went. You don't have to censor yourself with me or keep up this perfect façade." My weight balances on an elbow as I smooth amber tendrils of hair out of her face, needing her to read the sincerity in my eyes. "You're wound so tight, Kenzie. So focused on never taking a misstep. Afraid if you let go that you'll shatter into a million little pieces with no one to help put you back together again, but you have me. I will search and crawl with hands scraped and bloody for every last shard to prove you're not alone. I will be here to fit the pieces back together, to hold you safe."

She tries to turn her head away, but I hold firm, determined that she let my words sink in.

"But I don't want to shatter. The cracking I received when Kyle broke up with me was more than enough. The fractures I got when my first business venture tanked because my friend and business partner failed to uphold her side of things was *more than enough.*" Each word falls with fervor and one of her hands grips my bicep as if to shake sense into me. "Right now, you say you'll be there, but people change. They can be unreliable. Marriages of twenty years end because someone wakes up one day and decides they don't fucking love their spouse anymore. Nothing is guaranteed, so why should I stop trying to make the best of every situation I'm in by controlling what I can?"

"Because it's not making you happy," I state simply. "Because eventually something will fall through, and you know what? You'll pick yourself up and survive it. Because you're a strong fucking woman." My hand tightens in her hair, matching her in intensity. "Nothing's guaranteed, buttercup, except for you and me. And if, God forbid, that ever changes, the time we spent together would've been worth it. I would still choose to love you all over again despite knowing how it ends."

"You can't possibly know that. You don't love me, yet."

"Don't I?" Letting my body crush hers into the mattress, I quell any rebuttal with a harsh kiss of possession.

Love at first sight seemed like a fairytale. Love in a weekend seemed only marginally more realistic. Yet Kenzie's shown me the error of those beliefs. I love her. As crazy as it sounds.

I love her enough to wait until she feels safe enough to express the same emotion.

"No," she mutters, daring me to force her submission, her acceptance.

"Guess it's time to find out who's right, then."

Shifting over her, I shimmy out of my boxer briefs and guide Kenzie to her right side before straddling one leg and wrapping the other around my hip, allowing me more access to her body. "I'm going to fuck this cunt until you believe every word I've said. You don't have to admit to loving me yet, but you sure as hell are going to acknowledge my feelings for you." My fingers pluck at her nipples and clit, preparing her for a rough ride.

"Because sex is the answer?" She laughs in astonishment. "It's not a magic pill to life's problems."

Smack!

Her ass bounces from the light spanking. "Did I forget to mention I'll also be reddening these round cheeks to remind you who owns this curvy little body? You're mine, buttercup, even when you want to act like a brat." I punctuate the point with a hard thrust forward, driving through her wet pussy until she's taken all of me to the hilt.

A yelp of surprise erupts from Kenzie, and I pause, waiting to see if she'll use her safe word. When nothing else follows, I begin again—a steady rhythm of spanking her ass on every downthrust and pinching her clit on every retreat. I want her mindless with need. Lost in an ocean of battering, pleasure-filled waves with only me as her anchor.

She tries to grind into me, her nails clutching the wrinkled bedsheet in a white-knuckled grasp, but I refuse to let her assert any kind of control. Instinctively, I lean forward and capture the jiggling undercurve of her breast with my lips, sucking the delicate skin between my teeth as I tease her nipple with a damp finger covered in her arousal.

"Is this what you want, buttercup? What you need? To be stripped of responsibility? Of control?" A vibrating moan resounds in her throat, and her hand cups mine over her breast, squeezing the overflowing flesh, and it's the sexiest fucking thing I've ever seen. Her pale skin against the golden tones of my own. Kenzie touching herself through me—one of these days I'm just going to sit back and watch as she fucks herself in front of me. Glistening cunt open, her slim fingers pumping between their plump folds.

A spurt of pre-cum releases at the image, so I focus on my breathing—one, two, three—determined not to come until she does.

"No..."

Now, she's just being contrary.

With a devilish grin, I give her two spankings in quick succession and barrel forward with a thrust of my hips. She's going to learn every ridge of my cock before this weekend ends. Be imprinted by the steel length, so it's the only one she wants.

Kenzie's going to fall in love with my cock.

Then she's going to fall in love with me.

A flimsy plan, but it's the only one I've got.

CHAPTER NINE

KENZIE

HE'S LOVING ME.

Fucking me.

Joel's fucking me to prove he loves me.

The gradual progression of thoughts is stilted and hazy, fighting through the sensory overload of being surrounded by Joel. His hands and mouth seem to be everywhere at once while his cock keeps plunging deep inside my pussy—in and out, in and out—a brutal pace that steals my breath away.

This isn't lovemaking... or at least, not what I've ever imagined it to be.

It's ownership. Possession. Reducing my world to one point: Joel.

Not this weekend. Not Kyle. Not what I need to do on Monday.

Just him.

And I could cry with relief.

I thought relationships had to be a certain way. I thought intimacy had to follow a certain path—a slow, steady trail of steps like I tried to enforce on our first kiss. The goal always to avoid heartbreak or feeling stupid by controlling as many factors as possible.

But I was wrong.

Joel has broken every single one of my rules—wrested control from my tired hands—yet I feel relieved, thankful. A weekend fling meant for fun turning into a life-changing experience because one former slacker decided to upend my world.

"Do you believe I love you?" The grunted question repeats in my head as I tilt my head to catch Joel's determined gaze, sweat dripping down his temples.

Do I?

"You want to be stuck with a control freak woman who can't relax?" It doesn't sound ideal, even if I am describing myself.

He slows his movements and draws a line down the center of my nose before tapping the end. "Are you kidding? Relaxing you will be one of my favorite pastimes, and I do a damned good job of it, too."

"If you do say so yourself..." I tease, battling my need for assurance and the desire to trust him. *You do trust him. You've trusted him, and he hasn't disappointed like you feared.*

No, he hasn't.

Joel followed through with his word and actions. The realization rips through my chest. Like falling off my bike on rainy asphalt at eleven years old. Breath sucked from my lungs. Speech impossible.

"You still haven't answered my question." Everything stops except for his thumb circling my clit, the strokes leisurely before gradually speeding up, and I follow the movement. *Round and round.* Unbearable need wracks my tense body. *Round and round.* Conflicting thoughts race through my exhausted mind. *Round and round.*

Stop, Kenzie.

Stop holding yourself back.

Stop hanging onto a million different threads of possibility, trying to weave them into the correct order.

Just stop.

And I let go with a heavy exhale.

A breathy "Yes" slides into a moan as my body shatters in pure contentment, all of Joel's persistence and attention culminating in a release of sheer bliss. I'm vaguely aware of a few erratic thrusts before he joins me with a growl, his large body collapsing behind my back to spoon around me, but for once, I'm not obsessed with thinking or planning or wondering what's next.

Instead, I'm floating. Like a dandelion in the wind, waiting for the wind to carry me home.

We drift together peacefully as muffled voices filter in from the hall. As the glow of lights outside seep through the heavy curtains. We drift and make love again. Drift. Sleep. Drift. Fuck.

Hours pass in a blur of pleasure, and I'm content.

Until Joel breaks the silence with a quiet observation. "I'm surprised you didn't freak about the lack of protection."

An unladylike snort erupts before a full-blown bout of laughter explodes from my chest. Giggling, I turn my face towards him and grin. "That's cute and a little late for concern. You think I'm not on the pill?" With all of my talk about control and responsibility, I definitely don't take chances with pregnancy or getting surprised by my period.

"Right." He chuckles, tugging on a loose strand of my hair. "Control issues."

I peck his cheek because he's adorable and sweet, and I just can't resist. Haven't been able to resist much this weekend when it comes to him, honestly. The two sides of Joel—rough then tender, serious then playful—are very appealing to me, which I suppose is a good thing considering how he loves me and all.

God, I can't believe it.

But I know it's true, however improbable I would've found it two days ago.

"You know you love me," I say, testing the words out—still needing to get used to hearing it, despite Joel literally spelling it out on my skin with his mouth and fingers with every skillful touch.

"Mmm... I do." He leans forward for another kiss when my phone pings with an incoming message, reminding me of the world outside our bubble.

"Hold that thought." Twisting around to grab my phone from the nightstand, I see Emily's smiling face appear on the screen with a text.

Hey, are you okay? We're missing you at the dance.

Joel's lips drift down my spine reminding me of just how *okay* I am. We haven't left this bed for much more than a shower or grabbing the food delivered to the hotel room in the past twenty-four hours.

I'm sore in muscles I didn't even know I had, yet also strangely calm. *Zen.* My mind's not racing with worry over not helping at the dance tonight or organizing a list of tasks to do before tomorrow's awards brunch. It's as if Joel taking the reins in bed and displaying his competency has taught me that giving up a little control isn't so bad after all.

Clearly the dance is going off without a hitch since Emily's only concern is my absence.

I'm fine. I'll tell you about it tomorrow after brunch.

With a busy weekend ahead of us, we'd decided beforehand to reserve our last afternoon on campus for the girl talk we've been missing. And boy do we have a lot to talk about.

"Everything alright?" Joel asks, nuzzling into the small of my back.

"Yeah, just Emily wondering why I'm missing the dance." Returning to my previous position, I rest my head in a pillow and close my eyes, basking in the tender kisses and soothing massage Joel bestows upon me. He really should make gentle lovemaking his default because he's so damn good at it.

Yeah, but his dominant fucking isn't so bad either.

My thighs tighten in remembrance, and a labored groan unwillingly follows as I acknowledge the fact that I won't be up for such rigorous activity for a while.

I really need to start stretching more.

"I think I'm going to run you a hot bath to help relax your muscles, buttercup. It doesn't sound like you're feeling better."

"A bath would be heavenly, though I feel wonderful. This is a good sort of pain. Like the sense of achievement you feel after running a marathon... or at least I imagine this is how it feels."

Joel snickers and kisses my shoulder before the bed shifts, and the rush of water hitting tile echoes from the bathroom. I could get used to this kind of pampering. Amazing sex and amazing after-care.

I don't know the logistics of how we're going to continue our relationship past this weekend, but I *do* trust that we are continuing it. Joel's too devoted, determined to make a plan—whatever it may entail—and I'm satisfied with following his lead, trusting him.

Trusting his love.

And trusting yours.

Because I'm falling for him, probably already there, though I'm not brave enough to admit it aloud. But I will. Eventually.

Maybe even by the end of this weekend...

I bury a silly smile in my pillow and revel in the possibilities.

In the freedom of a future with Joel.

EPILOGUE ONE

JOEL
ONE YEAR LATER

I LOVE MY LIFE.

After a hectic twelve months, Kenzie and I are finally settled into our new home in my hometown, and we can ditch long-distance for good. Sure, it made for some sexy late-night phone calls, but I much prefer having my girl within kissing distance.

"Is that the last box?" Kenzie points to the plastic container I sit on the kitchen counter as she continues organizing our cabinets with dividers and labels—my little control queen putting her professional talents to work.

"Yep, we're officially moved in."

"Thank God. And you, your brother, and your father for hauling everything inside." She carefully unwraps a set of plates before moving onto matching bowls. "You know, your mom and I gladly would've helped."

"I know, but we had it covered." Easing behind her, I squeeze her waist, adoring the way her body cushions me in softness. The nape of her neck draws my attention, tiny wisps of hair escaping her ponytail, and my lips unerringly land on the delicate column. "Besides, it's only fair when you're the one who moved across the country."

We talked then fought then talked some more about who should move. I was more than willing to do whatever was necessary to be near her, but Kenzie defended her stance and won like a debate champion. She could run her business from anywhere; it wasn't tied to one location. One of her trusted employees would be promoted to care for the clients they had locally while Kenzie would network to build a second list of clients in her new home.

"You don't owe me for that. I'm happy to be here with you and your family. I know what your family's practice means to you. You love it, and I love you. So, the decision was simple."

Nipping at her ear, I whisper, "Say it again."

"I love you."

I'll never tire of hearing those three words from her pretty lips. Each time is a gift, especially when I know how difficult it was for her to let go and open herself to me—to give up control.

"Love you, too, buttercup... Why don't you forget organizing the kitchen, and I'll show you just how much?"

"Where?" Kenzie chuckles, escaping my hold. "Our bed isn't set up yet."

"Wherever I catch you." I grin and brace as if at a starting line. "You've got five seconds. One, two..."

A squeak of excitement pierces the air, and she takes off, her laughter fading as she gets further away. *Yeah, my girl's ready to play*, I think smugly.

"Five!" I shout.

Let the games begin.

EPILOGUE TWO

KENZIE
NINE YEARS LATER

"HOW'S IT FEEL TO NOT be responsible for all of this?" Joel waves a hand towards the outdoor carnival erected next to campus. This year the alumni committee decided to combine each class's resources and celebrate one giant reunion in conjunction with homecoming, and I'm relieved that he encouraged me to step down from the committee two years ago, so I didn't have to organize this.

While I love Trinity and will always help where I can, it eventually became too much—especially once I was appointed as team leader. Everyone required my sign-off on every little thing. Something the old Kenzie would've loved, but the woman I've become absolutely hated. It dragged me back to that stress-filled place of balancing responsibilities and ensuring perfect outcomes.

A place I've worked hard to leave behind with Joel's encouragement along with my therapist's guidance.

"Wonderful. Now, I'm free to enjoy the carnival versus running around behind the scenes."

"Definitely a plus. Along with being available to make out with your husband like we're horny co-eds again." He drags me behind a caravan touting the world's best funnel cake and nuzzles into my hair.

"I was never a horny co-ed." I was too focused and stressed with schoolwork and extracurriculars.

"Ahh... my poor little wife. Tangled in a web of responsibilities. Good thing I rescued you when I did." He teases with a bite to my neck.

"Ten years tardy." I playfully shove him back with no success. "Don't leave visible marks. We're meeting up with Emily and Landon tonight, remember?"

"Em will be sporting her own set of love bites, and you know it. I can't be outdone by a former jock." The competition of one upmanship between Joel and Landon is as hilarious as it is ridiculous. *Men.*

Rolling my eyes, I tug on his hair in reprisal before moaning when he sucks that special spot right below my ear. *Damn.* Why does he know all of my turn-ons?

Because he's your husband. You should be used to his behavior by now.

Ten years together. Eight years married.

It's been a whirlwind of fun and love and learning to not take things too seriously. Joel is the perfect man for me—a man I never would've picked for myself when all I knew in life were the Kyles of the world. Thankfully, he barged in and stole my heart anyway.

Guess I shouldn't begrudge him those years he annoyed me in college. After all, his apology brought us together.

Brought me love and peace.

I couldn't have planned it any better myself.

THANKS FOR READING & DON'T FORGET TO RATE/ REVIEW!

Please consider leaving a rating/review on Amazon, Goodreads, Instagram, TikTok, and/or any other sites you review on.
Ratings & reviews are the #1 way to support an indie author like me.
They don't have to be long or even positive (though I hope you enjoyed this book!). All the algorithms care about are
QUANTITY.
The more reviews, the more my books are shown to other potential readers!
And they serve as guides to readers on whether or not to take a chance on an indie author.
I appreciate your support!

XO, Hallie

.

ABOUT THE AUTHOR

Hallie prefers steamy, insta-love stories where curvy girls are claimed by filthy-talking heroes. And when she ran out of reading material, she decided to write her own stories. If you want a quick, hot read, she's your girl!